Doing Our Part

Rosa Is a Good Student

James Samuel

illustrated by
Aurora Aguilera

PowerKiDS press™

New York

Published in 2019 by The Rosen Publishing Group, Inc.
29 East 21st Street, New York, NY 10010

First Edition

Editor: Elizabeth Krajnik
Art Director: Michael Flynn
Book Design: Raúl Rodriguez
Illustrator: Aurora Aguilera

Cataloging-in-Publication Data

Names: Samuel, James.
Title: Rosa is a good student / James Samuel.
Description: New York : PowerKids Press, 2019. | Series: Doing our part | Includes index.
Identifiers: ISBN 9781538345504 (pbk.) | ISBN 9781538343722 (library bound) | ISBN 9781538345511 (6pack)
Subjects: LCSH: School—Juvenile fiction.
Classification: LCC PZ7.S368 An 2019 | DDC [E]—dc23

Manufactured in the United States of America

CPSIA Compliance Information: Batch #CWPK19. For further information contact Rosen Publishing, New York, New York at 1-800-237-9932

Contents

Rosa loves going to school!
She likes to learn.

Rosa tries to be a
good student.

She gets to school on time.

Rosa puts her things away quickly.

Then she sits at her table.

First, the class works on writing.

Rosa likes this part!

11

Next, the class works on adding.

Rosa doesn't like math.

13

Rosa works hard to get better.

She got all her math problems right!

After lunch, the class reads.
Rosa loves books.

17

It's computer time!

Rosa listens
to her teacher.

19

Rosa listens to directions.
She follows the steps.

22

Rosa is a good student.
She loves to learn!

23

Words to Know

book

computer

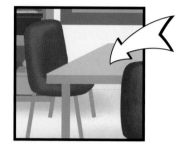
table

Index